D0065829

Ruby Bakes a Cake

Ruby Bakes a Cake

by Susan Hill

pictures by Margie Moore

HarperCollinsPublishers

Ruby Bakes a Cake

www.harperchildrens.com

Library of Congress Cataloging-in-Publication Data
Hill, Susan.
Ruby bakes a cake / story by Susan Hill ; pictures by Margie Moore.—1st ed.
p. cm. — (I can read book)
Summary: Ruby Raccoon asks her friends for advice on making a cake.
ISBN 0-06-008975-X — ISBN 0-06-008976-8 (lib. bdg.)
[1. Cake—Fiction. 2. Friendship—Fiction. 3. Raccoons—Fiction. 4. Animals—Fiction.]
I. Moore, Margie, ill. II. Title. III. Series.
PZ7.H5574 Ru 2004
[E]—dc21

2002012740

1 2 3 4 5 6 7 8 9 10
❖
First Edition

For Molly
—S.H.

For Jessie
—M.M.

FLOU
XXXX

Ruby Raccoon wanted
to bake a cake,
but she didn't know how.
"I will ask my friends
what it takes
to bake a cake," she said.

Ruby ran to the stone wall.

She saw Sam Squirrel.

“Sam, what does it take

to bake a cake?”

"Try adding nuts," said Sam.

"Thank you!" said Ruby.

"Come join me

when my cake is done!"

Ruby ran to the fence.
She saw Bunny Rabbit.
"Bunny, what does it take
to bake a cake?"
"Every cake needs carrot tops,"
said Bunny.
"Thank you!" called Ruby.
"Please come over
when my cake is done!"

Ruby ran to the brook.

She saw Dan Duck.

“Dan, what does it take

to bake a cake?”

"I never made a cake,

but I always enjoy snails," said Dan.

"Thank you!" said Ruby.

"Please come to my house

when my cake is done!"

Ruby ran to the tree.

She saw Jenny Wren.

"Jenny, what does it take

to bake a cake?"

"Don't forget wiggly worms,"

said Jenny.

"Thank you very much!"

called Ruby.

"Please come over

when my cake is done!"

Ruby ran to the pond.

She saw Frankie Frog.

“Frankie, what does it take

to bake a cake?”

Flick. *Flick*. "Flies," said Frankie.

"Really?" said Ruby.

"Well, please join me

when my cake is done!"

Ruby ran home.

She put everything into a big bowl.

She mixed the batter up

and put it in a pan.

She baked it in the oven.

“This does not smell good,”

said Ruby.

Ruby's friends came to share her cake.

She took it out of the oven.

“This does not look good,”

said Ruby.

Ruby cut the cake.

She gave it to her friends.

Her friends began to eat.

"This does not taste good,"

said Ruby.

“No, no, Ruby,

the cake is nice and crunchy,”

said Sam.

“And the cake is good and tall,”

said Bunny.

"It has a lovely round shape,"

said Dan.

“I have never tasted
such a juicy cake,”
said Jenny.

“And what a color, Ruby!”

said Frankie.

“This is one green cake.”

Ruby smiled.

“It is not a good cake,” she said.

"But you are very good friends."